Sleepover Girls Go Karting

by Narinder Dhami

Collins

An imprint of HarperCollins*Publishers*

First published in Great Britain by Collins in 2001
Collins is an imprint of HarperCollins*Publishers* Ltd
77-85 Fulham Palace Road, Hammersmith,
London, W6 8JB

The HarperCollins website address is
www.harpercollins.co.uk

3 5 7 9 8 6 4

ISBN 0 00710629 7

Printed and bound in Great Britain by
Clays Ltd, St Ives plc

Sleepover Kit List

1. Sleeping bag
2. Pillow
3. Pyjamas or a nightdress
4. Slippers
5. Toothbrush, toothpaste, soap etc
6. Towel
7. Teddy
8. A creepy story
9. Food for a midnight feast:
   chocolate, crisps, sweets, biscuits.
   In fact anything you like to eat.
10. Torch
11. Hairbrush
12. Hair things like a bobble or hairband,
    if you need them
13. Clean knickers and socks
14. Change of clothes for the next day
15. Sleepover diary and membership card

CHAPTER ONE

"I'll tell you what," I said. "Why don't we glue all the Watson-Wades' windows and doors shut so they can't get out? Or we could parachute on to their roof, and drop stinkbombs down the chimney. Or we could dress up in white sheets and haunt them?"

Frankie grinned, and poked me in the ribs with her elbow. "You're always so full of good ideas, Kenny!" she said.

"You know me," I said modestly. "If you want a good idea, I'm the main man!"

"Yeah, wasn't it *your* idea to try and decorate my bedroom?" Rosie said thoughtfully. "We got banned from having any more sleepovers for a while after that."

"And it was *your* idea to have that stupid bet with the M&Ms when we went to Disneyland, Paris," Fliss chimed in. "We nearly got trashed by our worst enemies!"

"Never mind, Kenny," Lyndz said kindly. "You do have really good idea sometimes…"

Aah, that's Lyndz all over. She wants to be nice to *everybody*.

"… It's just that I can't think of any at the moment!" she finished.

Yep, these guys are my *best* mates! With friends like these, who needs enemies? Only kidding. Our *real* enemies are the snotty old M&Ms, but you probably already know all about *them*, and they're not in this story anyway, so we can forget all about them (hurrah!).

Anyway, let's get on with it! I've got this *really* coo-ell story to tell you all about what we did at half-term. You'll never believe what happened. We had a fab time and—

Hang on a minute. What do you mean, you don't know who we are? You mean to say there's at least *one* person in the world who hasn't heard of the mega-fantastic, ultra-cool, completely class Sleepover Club???

Oh. Apparently there *is* one person who's never heard of us. OK, for that person's benefit, here's the rundown. I suppose you can sort of guess why we're called the Sleepover Club, can't you? 'Cos we sleep over at each other's houses, of course – duh! There's me, Kenny (or you can call me Laura if you really want to wind me up), Frankie, Rosie, Lyndz and Fliss. You'll figure us all out as we go along, I expect.

Anyway, it was half-term, and we were sitting in the Proudloves' garden. That's Fliss's family, if you didn't know. She used to be called Sidebotham, poor thing –but now her mum's remarried, thank goodness! We were having a sleepover at Fliss's that night. Mind you, we'd be lucky if we got any sleep. Fliss's mum has just had twins called Joe and Hannah, and they cry a lot. That's why the Proudloves' neighbours, the Watson-Wades (or the Grumpies, as we call them) had been moaning. Mrs Proudlove was really getting ratty about it, which was winding Fliss up – and when Fliss is wound up, the rest of the Sleepover Club really know about it! So I was trying to think how we could get our revenge.

"We could climb over the fence and steal their fish!" I suggested with an evil grin. "That'd really annoy them."

We all looked over into the Grumpies' garden. They had a really posh pond with gold and silver fish in it, and lots of plants around the edge. I don't know if you remember because it was ages ago, but when we had a sleepover at Fliss's once, we burnt a whole load of toast and chucked it over the fence into the Watson-Wades' pond to get rid of it! They were not pleased.

"And what would we do with the poor old fish?" Frankie asked. "And don't say 'eat them'!"

Frankie's a veggie, remember?

"We'd be doing them a favour," I pointed out. "We'd be saving them from the Watson-Wades!"

"Honestly, they're *so* grumpy, it just isn't true," Fliss groaned.

10

"Who, the fish?" I joked. "They seem pretty laid back to me, just swimming around there!"

"Oh, ha ha, Kenny, very funny." Fliss gave me a shove. "No, the Watson-Wades, of course. They moan *all* the time!"

"Yeah, it's a real pain." I winked at the others, who grinned. Fliss can moan for England herself if she puts her mind to it!

"I *mean*, babies cry," Fliss went on. "That's what they do!"

"And wet their nappies," Frankie added.

"And worse!" Lyndz said. She should know – she's got two baby brothers.

"Haven't the Grumpies got a baby of their own anyway?" I asked.

"Yeah." Fliss put on this really snooty voice. "Bruno Watson-Wade!"

"Your mum should go round and complain when *he* makes a noise, Fliss," Frankie suggested.

"*Boring*, Francesca Thomas!" I snorted. Frankie's far too sensible – well, some of the time. "I still think we should dress up and haunt them. That'd soon shut them up!"

"The Grumpies must be pretty weedy if they moan about the sound of a couple of babies crying," Rosie remarked. "It can't be *that* bad."

Right on cue, one of the twins started crying inside the house. A few seconds later the other one joined in. They were both yelling at the top of their lungs, and it sounded like ten cats screeching their heads off at the same time. It *was* pretty deafening.

"See?" Fliss yelled over the racket. "It's not *that* bad, is it?"

"NO!" we all shouted back. I dunno about the others, but I was dying to put my hands over my ears!

Fliss's mum appeared at the French windows.

"Fliss!" she yelled. "Could you come in and keep an eye on the pasta, while I see to the twins?"

"All right, Mum!" Fliss yelled back. So we all trooped inside and into the kitchen, where the spaghetti was boiling away on the cooker. Luckily, after a few minutes the screaming stopped.

"We can play with the babies after tea if you like," Fliss offered.

"Yeah, good idea," Rosie said eagerly. Frankie, Lyndz and me didn't look that keen, though. Rosie hasn't got any babies at home, that's why she's so up for it. But Frankie and Lyndz both have, and as for me, I'm just not that that interested. I only like people who can talk, and are toilet-trained.

"So what are we going to do with the rest of this half-term, then?" Frankie asked, taking charge as usual.

Everyone looked at each other.

"Have a couple more sleepovers," Lyndz suggested. We're not allowed to have sleepovers during the week in term-time, so we were making the most of the holiday by packing in as many as possible.

"Yes, but what else?" I asked impatiently. "I wanna do something exciting. Something interesting. Something I've never, ever done before…"

"Be sensible?" Rosie said, deadpan.

The others fell about. Rosie's jokes can sometimes really get you where it hurts!

Right at that moment we heard the sound of the front door slam, and a few moments later Andy came into the kitchen. He's not Fliss's real dad, but he's OK. Andy's a plasterer and he'd just got in from work, so he was still in his dusty overalls.

"Hi, girls," he said, going over to the fridge. "I don't suppose any of you are interested in karting?"

I didn't think I'd heard him right, so I just stared at him. So did all the others.

"*What* did you say, Andy?" Fliss asked.

"I said, are any of you interested in karting?" Andy took a can of beer out of the fridge, and popped it open.

"What, in a horse and cart?" Rosie asked, looking confused.

"No, you twit!" Frankie said. "He means go-karting."

Andy nodded. "Yeah, go-karting." He looked round at us. "So, are you interested?"

"You bet," I said eagerly. "I can just see myself burning rubber like Michael Shoemaker or whatever his name is!"

"Schumacher," Frankie corrected me.

"Sounds like a laugh!"

"I've never done it before, but I'll give it a go," Lyndz said.

"Me too," Rosie agreed.

"Don't you have to wear a safety helmet?" Fliss asked anxiously. "It might ruin my hair!"

The rest of us groaned.

"Come on, Fliss, get a life," I ordered. "Stop being so girly!"

"Oh, all right," Fliss retorted. "Anyway, isn't karting expensive?"

"Yeah, it is," Andy agreed, "if you haven't got free passes!" And he pulled five green tickets out of his pocket and held them up. "Here we are – five free three-day passes to the brand-new Silver Streak karting centre, starting tomorrow."

Our eyes nearly popped out of our heads.

"Three days of karting – brilliant!" Frankie gasped.

"Do you think we'll have races?" Lyndz asked.

"And do you think we'll need any special clothes?" Rosie chimed in.

15

"I hope my kart's pink." That was Fliss, of course!

"Cool!" I exclaimed, grabbing one of the passes and studying it. "Where did you get them from, Andy?"

Andy grinned. "I'm doing some plastering for a Mr Stevens at the moment," he explained. "He's got a big house in the country, and pots of money. He owns the karting centre, and he offered me the passes. The centre's only been open a few days, and I think he's a bit worried no-one's going to turn up!"

Just then Mrs Proudlove bustled into the kitchen with a baby in each arm.

"Andy, Joe and Hannah both need changing," she said, looking harassed. "Can you give me a hand?"

"I think this is where the Sleepover Club disappears!" I muttered to Frankie, and we all legged it into the living room.

"And it's Kenny in the blue kart who takes the lead," I announced, as I swerved ahead of Rosie, and elbowed her out of the doorway. "And it's Kenny who's first into the living room, and first into the comfy chair!" I sat

16

down in the armchair, and grinned at the others. "I'm gonna blow you all off the track tomorrow!"

"Knowing you, you'll probably crash into something!" Fliss sniffed.

"Or turn your kart over," Frankie added.

"Hey, I wonder if you can do stunts in those karts?" I said eagerly. "Maybe I'll be able to do a wheelie or something."

"If you do, you'll be *wheelie* lucky!" Frankie joked, and the rest of us bombarded her with cushions.

"I'll get my mum to take us tomorrow," I offered. "She's not doing anything. Well, even if she is, I'll get round her somehow."

"I hope they show us how to drive the karts," Fliss said anxiously. "I've never been in one before."

"Oh, it'll be cool!" I assured her. "It'll be just like driving a dodgem car at the fair."

"Oh yeah?" said Lyndz. "Remember *last* time we were on the dodgem cars?"

"That was an accident," I said with dignity. "I didn't *mean* to hit that other car so hard that the little boy lost his toffee apple."

"Yeah, but I don't think that woman who got it in the face was very pleased," Frankie pointed out.

"You're just jealous of me because I'm the best driver!" I boasted. "You wait and see!"

CHAPTER TWO

"And Mrs McKenzie's right at the back of the queue!" I was pretending I was talking into an imaginary microphone, and the others, who were squashed into the back of the car, were laughing their heads off. "If she doesn't put her foot down and spin some wheels, we won't even make it to the karting centre before it closes!"

"And if Laura McKenzie doesn't shut up," my mum replied calmly, as she stopped at some traffic lights, "she won't even make it to the karting centre, full stop."

"Oh, come on, Mum," I pleaded. "Can't you

19

go a bit faster? You've got no chance of winning a Grand Prix!"

"I can see you're going to be a great driver, Kenny," my mum said sarcastically as we drove out of Cuddington. "If you come home in one piece, I'll be surprised!"

"Don't worry, Mrs McKenzie," Rosie chimed in. "We can carry Kenny back to the car if we have to!"

"Listen, you lot, it takes skill to drive a kart," I snorted. "And I've got plenty of it!"

Secretly, I didn't have a *clue* what driving a kart involved – but I wasn't going to tell the others that. After all, how hard could it be?

"I'm not looking forward to wearing a helmet," Fliss moaned. "I bet it won't go with my new jumper!"

"Oh, give it up, Flissy," I retorted. "It won't matter anyway – we have to wear race suits over our clothes."

"What are those?" Lyndz asked.

"These kind of all-in-one overall things," I said airily. My dad had bought a computer last month, and I'd done a bit of research into karting on the Net the night before.

"Well, I hope mine's pink!" Fliss said, and everyone groaned.

"I think we have to wear gloves too," Frankie added, winking at me. "You're not the only one who went on the Net last night, Kenny!"

The karting centre was about fifteen miles from Cuddington. None of us quite knew what to expect, so when we arrived at the Silver Streak about twenty minutes later, we could hardly believe our eyes.

"Is that it?" Fliss gasped.

"It's *huge!*" Rosie murmured, her eyes almost popping out of her head.

It was *massive*. The building was shaped a bit like a big dome, and there was a large carpark outside, which already had quite a few cars parked in it.

Silver Streak Karting Centre

"Look!" Lyndz pointed at the big sign, as we drove into the carpark. "It says there's an adults' track, and a separate track for the under-elevens."

21

"Come on, Mum!" I yelled, bouncing up and down in my seat. I was getting well excited by now. "Put your foot down, and grab that empty parking space before that Mercedes gets it!"

"Oh, really, Kenny!" my mum said sternly. She reversed neatly into the empty space, just ahead of the Mercedes, and I cheered loudly. "I dread to think what you're going to be like what you get on to that karting track."

"Yeah, Kenny, haven't you heard of road rage?" Fliss said.

"Or in this case, *track* rage!" Frankie grinned.

"Yeah, you lot had better stay out of my way," I said, climbing out of the car. "If we have a race, I'm out to win!"

Frankie turned to Fliss.

"I bet you 50p Kenny crashes her kart," she said confidently, holding out her hand. "Shake on it?"

"No, thanks," Fliss retorted. "I can't afford to lose 50p!"

"What a cheek!" I grumbled, as we went over to the entrance. "I'm going to be the fastest out of you lot."

"I reckon Frankie will be a good driver," Lyndz said. "She was the only one who didn't get bumped when we went on the dodgems."

"I think Fliss could be quite good," Frankie remarked, "if she stops worrying about her hairdo for five minutes!"

"Well, I reckon Lyndz is going to be the best," Rosie added. "She's always good at things like this."

"Mum, have you got those free passes?" I asked impatiently, as we went up to the ticket office.

My mum stared at me. "No, I thought Fliss gave them to you."

"What!" I howled. "She did – but then I thought I gave them to you to look after! Oh no, that means we'll have to go back home for them—"

"Oh, wait a minute." My mum grinned at me, and then pulled them out of her handbag. "Here they are."

I glared at her while the others roared.

"Looks like you're not the only queen of the wind-up, Kenny!" Frankie spluttered.

"Oh, very funny, Mum!" I said crossly, as

we went into the arena. Then I stopped and stared round. "*Wow!* Hey, you guys, look at this!"

There were karts hurtling round the tracks, right before our eyes. The track close to us was the kids' one, and the adults' track was on the other side of the building. The tracks weren't just straight and flat, they had lots of bends as well as ramps leading up to bridges. They were surrounded by these banks, which must have been there to stop the karts coming off. There were men in overalls with flags, standing at the side watching everything that was going on – I think they were the race marshalls. The noise was pretty loud, but it looked incredibly exciting. I couldn't wait to be out there doing exactly the same thing!

"Look, there's a café and a restaurant as well," Lyndz said as we made our way further into the arena.

"And somewhere for spectators," Frankie added, pointing at a large, fenced-off area filled with seating.

"You'll be able to sit there and watch us, Mum," I said eagerly.

"Yes, and I've brought a book to read in case I get bored," my mum replied.

"Bored!" I repeated, amazed. "How could anyone get bored watching the Sleepover Club go karting?"

Parents! Don't you just love 'em?

"Well, I'll try not to," my mum said with a grin. "I'm off to have a cup of tea in the café. The girl at the ticket office said you're to wait here, and someone will be along to get you kitted up and give you some driving instruction before you're allowed out on the track."

Fliss was looking a bit sick as my mum went off.

"Those karts go really fast, don't they?" she muttered. "What if I can't keep up?"

"And look, this is only a practice session," Lyndz pointed out, glancing up. An illuminated board above our heads was flashing the words *Practice Session* at us. "It's not even a race."

"Don't worry, Flissy," I said. "I'll just give you a bit of a bump up the backside with my kart!"

"Don't you dare, Kenny!" Fliss squealed.

"Yeah, Kenny, this isn't the dodgem cars now," Frankie chimed in.

"You'll probably get thrown off the track if you do something like that," Rosie added.

We stood there watching the karts zoom round the track. There were eight of them going round, and there was one which was always at the front. It looked very different from the other karts, which were red, blue, green and white. This kart was black with gold flashes on it, and the driver was wearing a black race suit and a black helmet with gold writing on the front, which read *King of the Track*.

I nudged Frankie.

"Seen that one?" I pointed it out. "Bit flash, isn't it?"

Frankie nodded. "I wonder who it is?"

Just then one of the race marshalls jumped out and waved a chequered flag. The karts started pulling off the track into the pit stop, the black and gold one at the front.

"Come on," I said to the others. "Let's go and have a nose!"

We went over to the side of the track, and hung around watching what was going on. Mr *King of the Track* got out of his kart, and took his helmet off. He was about our age. He had dark hair, and the name *Josh* was embroidered on his black race suit in gold. I dunno why, but he looked really steaming mad!

"Hey, you!" He was glaring at another boy, who was just getting out of his kart. "Don't you know the rules? You're not supposed to race during a practice session!"

"I only tried to overtake you because you cut me up," the other boy retorted. "You were swinging about all over the place."

"Don't tell me what to do!" Josh snapped. "My dad owns this track, and I can get you banned from it any time I like!"

The other boy didn't say anything this time, he just stormed off. Meanwhile, our eyes were out on stalks.

"What a bighead!" I whispered to Frankie. "I'm surprised he can find a helmet to fit him!"

"Yeah, he really thinks he's something else, doesn't he?" she said, looking disgusted.

Fliss was looking worried. "I hope we don't have to race against *him*," she muttered.

"Look, he's having a go at someone else now," Rosie hissed.

"You're never going to be a good driver if you don't take risks, Alex," Josh was explaining in this snooty voice to one of the other drivers, a weedy-looking boy with red hair. "You've got to try and improve your cornering."

"I know," Alex said. "But it won't make much difference – your kart's so much faster than anyone else's."

A smug smile spread across Josh's already-smug face. "I know," he replied.

"Urgh!" I rolled my eyes at the others. "Pass me the sickbag, someone – and make it a giant-sized one!"

"Hi, girls." Josh had just noticed us all staring, and was looking down his nose at us. "Like the kart? It's mine, not the centre's. Brilliant, isn't it?"

"We're not looking at your kart – we're looking at you and wondering why you're such an annoying twit!" is what I *wanted* to say, but I didn't because Frankie kicked my ankle as soon as I opened my mouth. What I actually said was "Ow!"

"I'm Josh Stevens," Josh went on. "My dad owns this karting centre. And these are my two mates, Alex and Robin."

Robin was another weedy-looking kid with blond hair and specs. It was obvious that Josh *my dad owns this karting centre* Stevens liked having mates he could boss around, because they were both standing there looking up at him as if he was the best thing since sliced bread.

"So, girls." Josh said the word *girls* in a way that made me want to punch him on the nose. "Have you been karting before?"

I was dying to say that I was the World Under-Eleven Karting Champion, but I knew that would be a mistake. So I just said, "No."

"Oh, right." Josh grinned at us in this really annoying way. "Just take it slowly, and you'll be OK. It's not a sport for girls, really, anyway."

I clenched my fists. "Why not?"

"Kenny!" Frankie hissed in my ear, but I

took no notice. Meanwhile Rosie, Lyndz and Fliss had shuffled in closer to me, as if they thought they were going to have to hold me back from thumping the little creep. They were right!

"Well…" Josh shrugged his shoulders in this *incredibly* patronising way. "Everyone knows men are better at things like football and motor sport. Girls are better at things like netball and sewing!" He sniggered, and Alex and Robin sniggered too. "It's the same with karting. It's a man's sport!"

"Oh?" I said. "And is it a sport for slimy little creeps, too?"

Josh's mouth fell open, and his mates looked as if they were about to faint. "What did you say?"

"You heard me!" I snapped.

"And there are loads of girls here anyway," Frankie added, glancing round the arena. "There's no reason why girls can't be as good at karting as boys."

Josh looked down his nose at us. "That just goes to show you don't know anything about karting!" he sneered. "I've been karting

since I was five years old, and I'm an expert!"
Then he looked alarmed and took a step
backwards, as I took one forwards.

"We'll see!" I said, eyeballing him grimly.

"You've got no chance!" Josh retorted, and
then stalked off, with his two sheep – sorry,
mates – hurrying along behind him.

I turned to the others.

"Right, that's it!" I said firmly. "We've got to
show Mr Creep that girls are as good as
boys. We're all going to be *champion*
karters!"

CHAPTER THREE

OK, so the others moaned a bit, but they didn't really mean it. They hated Josh as much as I did. We were all determined to show him that he was talking rubbish, and that girls could be brilliant karters too.

Well, that was *before* we were taken off to be given driving instruction by Mike, the race director. There was so much to remember, it was almost impossible! First of all Mike took the five of us, plus some other kids, over to the beginners' area. There, we were given a number each, as well as safety helmets, gloves and race suits.

"Mine's too big," Fliss grumbled, as she rolled up her sleeves. "And it's not pink either!" she added sadly.

"Good," I retorted, as I struggled into my own race suit. "We don't want that idiot Josh thinking we're all weak and feeble girlies."

"He was the pits, wasn't he?" Frankie said. "Hey, guys, did you hear that? The pits – you know, the pit stop? That's a karting joke for you!"

"It's nowhere near a joke," I said. "It's not even funny! Look, we've got to show this creep just how wrong he is. So make sure you all listen up to Mike so you know what you're doing, OK?"

Everyone agreed, and there were lots of *woo hoo!*s and high fives. But when we finally got started, it was a different matter. Like I said, there was just *so* much to remember.

First of all, Mike showed us some of the karts. We all had the chance to sit in one and test out the pedals without actually moving.

"Now, unlike a proper car, there are only two pedals to worry about and no gears,"

Mike explained, pointing them out. "This is the brake, and that's the accelerator."

"I hope I don't mix them up!" Fliss whispered to me anxiously.

So did I. I could just see Fliss trying to brake, and going smack into the kart in front, headfirst. Josh Stevens would laugh himself silly!

Fliss looked even more worried when Mike explained that the karts could go up to thirty miles an hour. He told us that the steering wheel didn't turn very far, but turning it just a little had a big effect on how the kart moved. He also said that it was important to keep accelerating and not to slow down, as it was difficult to build up speed again. That made Fliss look even greener – I don't think she was looking forward to going fast at all!

We were given so many tips, my head was spinning by the end of it. You couldn't be too heavy on the brakes, especially if you were cornering, because then your kart might start twirling on the spot. I thought that sounded quite cool, but it wouldn't be if I was racing against Josh at the time. Then there were lots of hints about how to steer the kart round corners, and how to get the best acceleration. Then Mike went on for ages about the rules of the track, like moving over to let a faster kart get past you if the race marshall waves his flag, and not deliberately bumping into other people (that got you a black flag, which meant you were disqualified!).

By the end of it all, my head was ready to explode. The others were looking pretty dazed as well.

"I don't think I remember any of that," Frankie said.

"Do we really have to go at thirty miles an hour?" Fliss wailed.

"We'll never beat Josh and his mates," Lyndz groaned.

"We're going to be rubbish," Rosie said dismally.

"No, we're not!" I said firmly. "Come on you lot – we're the Sleepover Club, remember? We're not going to let that little toad get the better of us!"

So we all started woo-hooing and doing high fives again, as Mike led us over to the starting grid. The last practice session had just finished, and the karts were ready for us to have our first drive. Unfortunately, Josh and his mates were right there in the front row of the spectator area, watching us with big grins on their faces.

"Ignore them," I said to the others. "Just concentrate on driving— Ow!"

Great start. Fliss had just dropped her helmet, and it landed right on my toe.

"Sorry, Kenny," Fliss said, as we went over to our karts. "I'm a bit nervous."

"It's OK," I said through gritted teeth. Josh and his mates were rolling around having a right laugh. "Just keep calm, and you'll be fine." I was number 5, and I found my kart and climbed in. For one horrible second I couldn't remember which pedal was the brake and which one was the accelerator, but then it all came back to me. Phew!

"Good luck," Frankie called over to me. She was sitting in number 8, which was right next to me.

"Same to you," I called back, keeping an eye on the race marshall who was going to start us off. "Let's show that little creep Josh just how wrong he is!"

We didn't have time to say anything else, because the marshall was ready with his flag. I kept my eyes fixed on it until it dropped – and then we were away!

I put my foot down on the accelerator, and scorched away like I had a rocket up my bottom. No-one got *near* me as I zoomed off!

"I'm winning! I'm winning!" I grinned to myself. But next minute I got a black flag waved at me! Mike had said that if we were black-flagged, we *had* to leave the track, so sulkily I pulled off into the pit stop. As I did so, Frankie, Rosie and Lyndz roared past me. At least they were doing all right, although I couldn't see Fliss anywhere.

"Why did I get a black flag?" I asked crossly, pulling my helmet off as Mike ran over.

"Kenny, this is a *practice*," Mike said sternly. "You were warned beforehand to take it easy – no racing! You can go again in the practice session after this one."

"Oh." I felt a bit of an idiot. I'd completely forgotten the rule about not racing.

Then I spotted Fliss, in kart number 9. She was still sitting on the starting grid while everyone else was halfway round the track!

"What's the matter with Fliss?" I asked.

"She must have her steering lock on," Mike replied. "It's very difficult to get the kart to move from a standing position if the wheels aren't straight – ah, there she goes!"

Fliss was *finally* moving. I risked a quick look at Josh, although I knew it would wind me up. Him and his mates were red in the face from laughing. When Josh saw me looking, he gave me a mocking wave. I was dying to go over there and give him a slap!

Frankie, Rosie and Lyndz were doing OK, though, and so was Fliss now that she was on the move. Then, suddenly, everything went wrong for Rosie. She was heading towards one of the tight corners, and she was going pretty fast. Mike had warned us about braking hard when you turned corners, but Rosie had obviously forgotten. She hit the brakes and the kart went into a fast spin, twirling round and round several times, and then bumping into the bank at the side.

"Oh no!" I groaned, covering my eyes. This was a Sleepover Club disaster!

Lyndz was next to give Josh and his mates a good laugh. Somehow she got too close to the kart in front of her, and the front of Lyndz's kart hooked on to the back of the other one and she couldn't get it free. They drove round the track like that until the marshall made them come off and separate the karts.

Anyway, it turned out that Frankie and Fliss were our best drivers, although Fliss was a bit slow because she was nervous. But Frankie was ace! She was twisting and turning her way round those corners like she'd been karting for years.

"That was brill, Franks!" I said, when the practice session was over, and she and Fliss had pulled off the track along with the other drivers.

Frankie grinned. "I didn't do too badly, did I?"

"No, and nor did Fliss." I slapped Fliss on the back, as she took her helmet off. "Well done, Flissy!"

Fliss pulled a face. "I wasn't as good as Frankie. I didn't go fast enough."

"You will!" I assured her. "We'll all get better when we've practised a bit more."

"Enjoy your spin?" Josh was sauntering towards us with Alex and Robin. He grinned at Rosie, who turned red.

"Take no notice," Frankie said, grabbing my arm. "Kenny, I forbid you to attack him!"

"Spoilsport," I muttered, as Josh and his mates got closer.

"That was a great laugh!" Josh sniggered. "You girls should give up karting and take up comedy!"

"Shut up," I snapped. "We'll be loads better when we've practised a bit."

"Yeah, I bet *you* weren't much good either when you first started," Frankie added, glaring at Josh.

"Yeah, Josh, remember how you smashed up the very first kart your dad bought you—" Robin began. Then he turned pink as Josh glared at *him*. I reckon Robin was a bit like Alana Banana! You remember her, that dozy mate of the M&Ms in our class?

"I reckon you lot should give up and go home now," Josh remarked rudely. "Don't bother waiting for the races this afternoon."

"Races?" My ears pricked up at that. "What races?"

"We have races every day after the practice sessions," Josh explained in that smug voice of his. "There are six fifteen-lap heats, and the winner of each heat goes through to the final. The winner of the final gets a prize too." He grinned an evil grin. "Like I said, don't bother entering. You don't stand a chance!"

"Oh really?" I snapped. "Well, I can tell you this for nothing – one of *us* is going to win that final. You don't stand a chance!"

CHAPTER FOUR

"You've got a big mouth, Kenny!" Frankie groaned, as Josh and his mates sauntered off, laughing.

"Well, I couldn't let him have a go at us like that, could I?" I retorted. "It'll be cool. We'll do much better in the proper races."

The others looked at me doubtfully. Fliss was obviously scared to death, and Rosie and Lyndz looked like they were ready to go home. Even Frankie, who'd done so well, seemed pretty down.

"Oh, stop being such major wimps!" I said impatiently.

"We'll *never* beat that horrible Josh," Fliss said gloomily.

"We can *try*." I glanced over at Mum, who was sitting in the spectator area. "Come on, let's go and ask my mum if we can get a drink from the café. Looks like there's a few more practice sessions before the races start."

My mum smiled at us sympathetically as we went over to her. "Hi, girls," she said. "Well done, Frankie. Never mind, the rest of you. I'm sure you'll do better next time."

Fliss's face dropped even further, and Rosie and Lyndz both looked really depressed.

"Maybe we should just go home and forget the racing," Frankie suggested. "We can always try again tomorrow."

"No way!" I said firmly. "Josh'd laugh at us even more then! Is the Sleepover Club a bunch of wimps?"

"No," Frankie, Rosie and Lyndz muttered reluctantly. Fliss looked like she couldn't make her mind up, though!

We moved over to the café, and had some drinks and a big creamy cake each, which seemed to calm everybody down a bit. Then we went to find out which heat of the race we would be driving in. It turned out that me and Rosie would be in Heat 2 with one of Josh's weedy mates, Alex, while Frankie was in Heat 4. Lyndz and Fliss were drawn in Heat 3, along with Josh Stevens. Fliss nearly wet her knickers when she found out.

"Oh no!" she wailed. "I don't want to race against *him*!"

"You'll be fine, Fliss," I said, sounding a lot more confident than I felt. But I swear you could hear the noise of Fliss's knees knocking together, even over the sound of the karts!

The races were taken pretty seriously. There was even a race commentary on each heat which was broadcast over the tannoy, and made the whole thing even more exciting. We went over to watch Heat 1, which was won by the boy who'd had the row with Josh. Then it was mine and Rosie's turn.

"I'm scared!" Rosie muttered as we climbed into our karts.

"Don't panic," I replied. "Only one of us has to win, and we've got a Sleepover Club member into the final!"

"In your dreams!" said a rude voice. I looked round. Alex was standing by his kart, grinning at us.

"What're you laughing at?" I snapped, giving him the evil eye. Alex looked petrified, and jumped backwards as if I was about to attack him. What a weed!

"Will the drivers in Heat Two please take their places on the starting grid," said the commentator.

We all climbed into our karts. I looked across at Frankie and the others and waved as I revved my kart up. I could hardly wait to get started. It was a shame that we couldn't all go through to the final, but only the winner of each heat would make it.

I glued my eyes to the marshall at the side of the track who was holding the chequered flag. As soon as it dropped, my foot hit the accelerator and I was off like a rocket! It felt really cool to be going so fast.

"And kart number five is first away from the starting grid," I heard the commentator say as I headed towards the first bend. "Kart number fourteen is second, and kart three is third."

Rosie was in kart number 18, so she'd already fallen behind. I was dying to glance back over my shoulder to check it out, but as I was coming up to a sharp bend, I didn't dare.

"Right, don't brake," I muttered to myself as I swept round the corner. I remembered Mike telling us that the kart would slow down automatically when you were cornering, so only to use the brake when you came up to the bend, and not when you were actually going round it. To my complete amazement, I managed to get round the corner in one brilliant movement (even if I say so myself), and then I was on a straight bit of the track again – and I was still in front! I was really pleased with myself. In fact, I was so pleased that I decided to risk a quick glance back over my shoulder to see where Rosie was.

Big mistake. I dunno what happened, but just as I looked back, I lost control of my kart! I spun right round and stopped. My kart was stuck across the middle of the track, and the other karts were heading straight towards me!

"Help!" I yelled, desperately trying to get my kart moving again. But it wouldn't budge.

Luckily the other karts in the race, including Rosie, all managed to get round me, so there weren't any accidents. Then two marshalls ran on and helped me to point the wheels in the right direction and get the kart moving again. But I was *miles* behind everyone else. There was no way I was going to qualify for the semi-finals unless everyone else crashed out of the race.

"Go on, Rosie," I muttered as I drove under one of the bridges. "It's up to you now!"

Poor old Rosie wasn't doing so well, though. She was behind everyone else, and she didn't look like catching them up either. In fact, she was going so slowly that I almost caught up with her. We finally crossed the finishing line at almost exactly the same time. And we were both last.

Alex the Weed had won our heat, which was really sickening. By the time Rosie and I climbed out of our karts, Alex was already celebrating with Josh and Robin, doing high fives and grinning all over his stupid face.

"Better luck next time, girls!" Josh called smugly. If I'd still been in my kart, I would've run him over!

"Sorry, Kenny," Rosie muttered, as we left the track. "Karting's fun, but I don't think I'm ever going to be much good at it!"

"Yeah, well, I wasn't exactly brilliant either," I comforted her. "Let's hope Fliss and Lyndz can do better."

As we went over to join Frankie, who was still waiting her turn to race, Lyndz and Fliss came towards us, carrying their helmets.

"OK, it's up to you two now," I said. "Good luck!"

Lyndz looked really nervous, and Fliss looked as if she was about to faint! I couldn't help feeling a bit guilty. I mean, we were supposed to be having fun! If I hadn't gone on about beating Josh, we wouldn't have been so wound up, I guess.

"Look, just do your best," I said, trying to be nice. "Don't worry about beating that creep Stevens."

"Really?" Fliss looked relieved.

"Yeah. But if you *do* manage to beat him,

it'll be brilliant." You know me. I just couldn't help it!

Lyndz and Fliss grinned, and went over to their karts. Josh Stevens was already on the starting grid, fussing about the position his kart was in.

"I'd like to go over there and rip that stupid helmet right off his head!" I muttered to Frankie. "I mean, *King of the Track* – honestly!"

"The trouble is, he *is* pretty good," Frankie sighed.

"And he knows it!" I glared at Josh, who was now waving at his mates with an *I know I've won this already* look on his face.

So me, Frankie and Rosie got a REAL shock when the heat began. Josh roared off in front from the start, but guess who was right behind him? FLISS!

"Go, Flissy!" I yelled, dancing up and down as they went round the first bend. "Don't let him get away!"

Fliss was doing really well. She kept losing a bit of ground every time they went round a corner or a bend because Josh was more experienced, but then she'd make it up on the straight runs. Now they were heading for the bridge for the second time, and she was right behind him. Poor old Lyndz was way down the field in second-to-last place, but at least she was still going without any disasters.

"D'you think Fliss'll qualify for the next round?" Rosie asked anxiously, her eyes fixed to the track.

"There's still twelve laps to go," Frankie replied, "but she's got a great chance!"

By the eighth lap, Fliss was still right behind Josh. Until…

"Why is she slowing down?" I asked anxiously.

"Look, she's pulling off the track!" Frankie groaned. "There must be something wrong with her kart!"

We could hardly believe it. Fliss had had to drop out of the race because her kart had conked out. Honestly, I could have cried. And guess who won the race by a mile? Mr Smarmy Stevens, that's who!

"OK, Frankie," I said urgently, as the drivers for Heat 4 were called. "It's all up to you now."

"I'll do my best," Frankie promised. Then she slapped palms with each of us for luck, and went off to get into her kart. She looked pretty calm, but I'd already nearly chewed all my fingernails off by the time the race started.

Frankie drove brilliantly, but there was a girl in her heat who was pretty good. Frankie chased her all the way, with us screaming our heads off, but she couldn't catch her and she only made it into second place. It was a great result, but it wasn't good enough for her to get into the final. So there were *no* Sleepovers taking part at all. And didn't Josh Stevens just *love* it.

"Oh dear, girls!" he called, waving at us while Alex and Robin, who'd won Heat 6, stood around, sniggering. "Keep practising and you'll get better. In about ten years' time, maybe!"

That did it. I was steaming mad. I charged over to him – or at least I would have done if the others hadn't grabbed me and hung on. Frankie and Lyndz had hold of my arms, Fliss grabbed the collar of my race suit and Rosie flung her arms round my waist, and held on tight!

"OK, OK," I muttered crossly. "I won't kill him this time!"

"Maybe we'll do better tomorrow," Lyndz said hopefully.

Maybe she wasn't too wrong either. After all, Frankie and Fliss had turned out to be good drivers, and I wasn't too bad, as long as I didn't look over my shoulder! Lyndz and Rosie still needed a bit more practice, but we had two more days left on our free passes. If one of us could *just* beat Josh Stevens in just *one* race, it'd be brilliant…

Our karting session for the day was over. We could have stayed and watched the final, but none of us felt like it. After all, Josh Stevens was bound to win, and I'd had enough of his ugly mug to last me a lifetime!

"Where's your mum gone, Kenny?" Lyndz asked, as we came out of the changing area, having taken off all our racing gear.

"Dunno," I shrugged, and looked around. "She must be around somewhere. Maybe she's gone to the café again."

"Hey, guys!" That was Frankie, and she sounded really excited. "Come and look at this!"

There was a door standing open at the side of the arena, which led outside. Frankie was peering through it, and when we joined her, we saw what she was looking at. There were loads of old, beaten-up karts piled up in big heaps on the grass, some of them covered with tarpaulin.

"Come on, let's take a look," I said eagerly. I was about to rush through the door when Fliss grabbed my arm. "Look at the sign, Kenny."

I looked. There was a sign on the wall which read *Strictly No Entry for Members of the Public*.

"Oh, poo!" I scoffed. "Who's gonna know?" And I took a quick glance over my shoulder, and legged it outside. The others followed, although Fliss was worrying, as usual.

"What if Josh Stevens sees us?" she asked anxiously. "He might tell his dad!"

"Josh Stevens is too busy trying to win that race," I replied, as we heard the sound of the karts starting off again. "And anyway, we're OK. There's no-one out here."

"Hi, can I help you?" said a voice from behind us.

We all jumped two metres into the air, and Fliss actually screamed! There was a girl standing behind us, holding a screwdriver in her hand. She was a bit older than us, about fourteen, with long dark hair, and she was wearing scruffy jeans and a sweatshirt.

"Er – we just came out to look at the karts," I spluttered. "We didn't see the sign."

Frankie groaned and nudged me. "If you didn't see the sign, how do you know there *was* a sign?" she hissed.

I turned red, but the girl just laughed.

"Hi, I'm Charlotte, Charlie for short," she said with a friendly grin. "Are you interested in karts?"

"Well, we've only just started karting," Frankie explained. "But, yes, we are."

"Come and see mine," said Charlie, and she led us over to a really sad-looking kart. It wasn't even painted, it was just made of bare metal.

"Er – very nice," said Fliss awkwardly.

"Don't worry, I'm doing it up!" Charlie said with a grin. "I've just got to tinker with a few bits and pieces, and then I'll paint it."

"You're not going to paint it black and gold, are you?" I asked, winking at the others. "Because there's someone who might not be too pleased if you do!"

Charlie grinned even wider. "Oh, you've met Josh, I see."

"Yeah, worse luck!" I replied.

"He's a right creep," Frankie chimed in.

"And smug with it," Rosie added.

"He keeps winding us up," Lyndz explained.

"Do you know him?" Fliss asked.

"You could say that," Charlie replied. "He's my brother!'

We all nearly *died*. If a big hole had opened up right in front of us, we'd have jumped straight into it, I swear. We all started saying sorry, and that we didn't really mean it. Meanwhile, Charlie was laughing fit to bust.

"It's OK," she said. "I know he can be a right pain sometimes. He's been getting up my nose ever since Dad bought this place a few weeks ago."

"Are you into karting too, then?" Rosie asked.

Charlie nodded. "Yeah, I've been karting for years. But I prefer doing up old karts, while Josh likes to have the latest model on the market. That one he's driving at the moment cost a fortune."

"So what does Josh think about you karting?" Frankie asked. "He says it's a man's sport!"

Charlie shrugged. "Yeah, more boys than girls are into it, that's true. But the girls are just as good. Josh is just winding you up!"

"Hey, Kenny, we'd better get a move on." Frankie slapped me on the shoulder. "Your mum's probably looking for us."

"OK," I said reluctantly. I would've liked to stay and chat to Charlie a bit longer – she was cool!

"Are you coming on Saturday?" Charlie asked. "We've got a special race day on, with team races and prizes."

"Team races?" Frankie said, looking interested.

"Yeah, teams of five." Charlie grinned at us. "So you'll be OK!"

"Hear that, guys?" I said excitedly, as we waved goodbye to Charlie and went back into the arena. "The team races sound mega-cool!"

"And we've still got tomorrow to practise for them," Lyndz pointed out.

"Maybe we could all wear the same T-shirt or something on Saturday," Rosie suggested. "To show we're a team."

"Yeah, we could customise them with fabric paints," Fliss said. "Like we did when we played five-a-side football that time."

"We could do that tomorrow night when we sleep over at Lyndz's," Frankie added.

When we went back into the arena, there was some sort of presentation going on. There was a little stage to one side of the track, a bit like those platforms the medal-winners stand on in the Olympics, and Josh *Mr Smug* Stevens was standing on top of it, looking as if he'd just won a gold medal.

"Oh, knickers!" Frankie groaned. "He must've won the final!"

"Yeah, well, he won't be winning everything for much longer," I said confidently, "because the Sleepover Club is on hot on his trail!"

CHAPTER FIVE

"Uh-oh!" I nudged Frankie hard in the ribs with my elbow. "Creep alert! Pass it on!"

It was the following day, and we were back at the Silver Streak karting centre. My mum had moaned a bit about having to spend the morning there again, so this time she'd dropped us off and was coming back for us later. Meanwhile, we were all totally fired up about taking part in the team races on Saturday. We were taking our plain white T-shirts round to Lyndz's place tonight so that we could paint them, and we were going to discuss race tactics too (OK, so none of us *knew* very much about race tactics but it sounded good!).

Anyway, we'd just arrived in the arena when I spotted Josh. He was sitting in the café with a glass of Coke in front of him, and Alex and Robin were in the queue at the counter. We were all glaring at him when Josh happened to look round and see us. He grinned, and beckoned us over.

"Who does he think he is, the king?" I muttered, as we reluctantly went over to the rail which separated the café tables from the main arena. I would've ignored him, but I didn't want him to realise just how much he was winding us up.

"Well, I didn't expect to see *you* here today, girls," Josh said mockingly, raising his eyebrows. "I mean, you're obviously rubbish at karting! Why don't you just give up?"

"Why don't *you* go and play in the traffic?" I retorted.

"Not if you lot are driving!" Josh replied, and then laughed his head off as if he'd said something really funny.

"Hey, Josh." That was Robin calling from

the front of the café. "Do you want another Coke?"

Josh turned round. "Yeah, and get me a fudge brownie, a Crunchie and a Mars Bar. No, wait a sec, I'll have a Twix instead of a Crunchie."

While Josh was talking to Robin, he had his back to us. Quick as a flash, I leaned over the rail, grabbed the salt cellar off the table and up-ended it into his glass of Coke. I had just enough time to dump a whole lot of it in there before he turned back to us again. By the time he did, we were all standing there looking like butter wouldn't melt in our mouths.

"Like I told you, girls," Josh went on, "karting's for *boys*." He picked up his glass of Coke, and we all held our breath. "You could practise all day and you'd never be as good as me in a million years— URRRRGH!"

We all roared as Josh took a huge mouthful of Coke, pulled a disgusted face and then spat it out all over the table.

"That's horrible!" he spluttered furiously, wiping his mouth. "It tastes salty!"

By this time we were almost weeping with laughter. I was laughing so much I couldn't even stand up straight, and I had to hold on to Fliss because my knees were giving way.

"You did that!" Josh leapt to his feet, looking as if he was about to explode with rage. "You put salt in my drink!"

"Prove it!" I retorted coolly, as we all sauntered off, still grinning.

"Serves him right," Fliss said with satisfaction, as we heard Josh yelling at Alex and Robin to get him a glass of water.

"Brilliant move, Kenny!" Rosie slapped me on the back.

"Yeah, class, Kenny!" Lyndz agreed.

"That was one of your better ideas, Kenny," Frankie remarked.

"Thanks," I said modestly. Now all we had to do was beat Josh Stevens in today's races, and our revenge would be complete!

We had to wait a little while to take part in our first practice session as one had already started, so we went over to watch the action on the adult track for a bit. It was only a practice session, but there was one kart which was well ahead of the others all the time. The driver was really good, and when the kart pulled off into the pit stop, we realised that it was Charlie Stevens. So we went over to say hello.

"I'm just about to start painting my kart," Charlie explained, taking off her helmet and shaking her hair out. "D'you fancy giving me a hand for a bit?"

"Sure," I replied, and the others looked really keen too.

We followed Charlie outside. She'd already put the base coat on to the metal, so the kart was ready to paint.

"What colours are you using?" Rosie asked.

"Purple and silver," Charlie replied, prising the lids off the tins of paint with a screwdriver. "I thought I'd call it *Silver Flash*."

"Hey, my favourite colours!" Frankie grinned. "You could paint some lightning flashes on it, Charlie."

"Good idea," Charlie agreed.

While we were painting, we asked Charlie what would happen in the team races on Saturday. She told us that each member of the team would take part in two races each, and everyone got points, even if they came last. The team who got the most points overall would be the winner.

"So it's really important to keep trying hard, even if you're only third or fourth," Charlie explained. "The higher you finish, the more points your team gets."

"Will Josh be in the team races?" I asked, trying to finish off the part I was painting without getting any in Fliss's hair. She was crouched down in front of me doing a bit near the wheels.

"Oh yeah, with Alex and Robin and another couple of his mates." Charlie grinned at me. "I'll let you into a little secret. His other mates, Ben and Nathan, aren't as good at karting as Josh is."

"Oh, excellent!" I crowed. "That means we stand a better chance of beating them!"

"That's what we like about you, Kenny," Frankie remarked, carefully finishing off the bit she was doing. "You're such a good sport!"

"Fliss, what's that in your hair?" Rosie asked. "It looks like paint!"

"Kenny, you total idiot!" Fliss yelled, grabbing a rag and trying to clean herself up.

"Sorry, I got a bit over-excited," I said apologetically.

"Hey, why don't we all wear some hair mascara tomorrow as well?" Rosie suggested. "We could match it to our T-shirts."

"Oh, that's a great idea!" Fliss brightened up immediately, so I was off the hook. Phew!

We didn't have time to help Charlie finish the kart because our practice session was due to begin. But Charlie promised that, in return for our help, she'd give us some driving tips before the team races tomorrow. So we were all well pleased when we went back into the arena.

"I reckon we've got a great chance in these team races," I said eagerly. "Especially if Charlie's going to help us."

"Yeah, we can use today's individual races to practise for tomorrow," Frankie agreed.

Meanwhile, Rosie was looking gloomy. " I know I was the worst driver yesterday," she said. "I'm not going to score many points, am I?"

"I wasn't that brilliant either, Rosie," Lyndz said quickly. "So you know what I'm going to do? I'm going to pretend my kart's a horse!"

You know how crazy Lyndz is about horse-riding, but that was just a bit too weird! We all stared at her.

"Well, it's not *that* different, is it?" Lyndz muttered.

"Oh no, *every* horse has got a brake and an accelerator!" I grinned.

"And since when did you see a horse with a steering wheel attached to its neck?" Frankie snorted.

"OK, OK," Lyndz said, as we all fell about laughing. "But I still think it'll help."

"Just don't try giving your kart a lump of sugar!" I warned her, as we went over to get kitted up. Then Frankie grabbed my arm.

"Hey, guys," she said, a big grin spreading across her face as she pointed at the track. "Check it out!"

We all looked over at the track, where the last practice session was just finishing. Most of the karts had already pulled into the pit stop, but there were a few still completing their last lap. There was one kart right at the back which looked as if it was being driven by someone who hadn't got a *clue* what they were doing. The kart was going really slowly and weaving from side to side. The driver slowed down even more as they got near to a bend, so that the kart was practically crawling along. It was the worst bit of driving I'd ever seen.

"Oh, I *really* hope that driver's in my race tomorrow!" Rosie said longingly, as the kart pulled off the track. "I'll be able to beat them for sure!"

"A snail with a limp would beat that driver!" I said, disgusted. "I wonder who it is?"

We all watched curiously as the driver took her helmet off. Then we all groaned loudly. It was only Alana Banana Palmer, the doziest girl in our school!

"I might've known." Frankie rolled her eyes. "Only Alana Banana could drive like that!"

"I hope that doesn't mean the M&Ms are here!" Fliss said anxiously.

Alana Banana is kind of friendly with our big enemies, the M&Ms (otherwise known as the Gruesome Twosome), which is one reason why we don't like her very much. But Alana's generally a bit too dozy to seriously annoy us.

"No, it looks like she's here with her brother," Rosie said with relief, as Alana wandered over to a younger boy and a couple of other kids.

"Thank goodness," Lyndz sighed. "It would've been awful if we had to try and beat Josh Stevens *and* the M&Ms."

"Nah, it would've been cool!" I said confidently. "We're gonna do really well today – I can feel it in my bones!"

"Just don't break any, OK?" Frankie said jokingly.

Guess what? Our short practice session went brilliantly! Frankie and Fliss were definitely the best drivers, but I wasn't far behind, and even Lyndz and Rosie did much better. If pretending the kart was a horse meant Lyndz felt more at home, I didn't care how weird it was! OK, I admit that a lot of it had been just talk when I kept saying we were going to do well in the team races tomorrow, but now I was really beginning to feel that we had a chance. And now that the practice sessions were over, if we could do well in today's individual races it would give us a real boost for tomorrow.

"OK, guys," I said confidently, as we went to find out which heats we would all be racing in. "Let's go for it today, and see how many of us can get into the final!"

"I'll tell you how many," Smarmy Stevens' snooty voice chimed in from behind us. "Zilch!"

"Oh, it's you." I turned round, and smiled sweetly at him and his two sad mates. "Enjoy your Coke?"

Josh turned a sort of dark red colour, and stomped off without saying anything.

"You shouldn't wind Josh up like that," Alex said accusingly.

"Why not?" I said. "I enjoy it!"

"Josh'll be out to get you now!" Robin said, and then the two of them rushed after him.

Frankie frowned. "I don't like the sound of that."

"Oh, relax, Franks," I shrugged. "They're just trying to annoy us. What can Josh Stevens do to us?"

Good question...

CHAPTER SIX

"Oh, rats!" I groaned, as I shot across the finishing line in second place. I'd had a great drive and done well, but I needed to be first in the heat to qualify for a place in the final. I'd just missed out – and so had Rosie, who was in the same heat as me. She was just coming in, in fourth place.

"Bad luck, Kenny," Rosie panted, as we took our helmets off. "You were so close!"

"I know," I said gloomily.

"Never mind, at least we've got a good chance in the team competition tomorrow," Rosie pointed out, as we went over to join the others. "We're all doing much better today."

It was true. Fliss and Lyndz had gone in the heat before us, and Lyndz had come third and Fliss was actually second. Mind you, I could have sworn I saw Lyndz stroking her kart before the race started, and whispering things to it.

Snooty Stevens had gone through to the final, of course, and so had his mate Robin. Alana Banana had crashed out of her heat though, and had nearly taken half the other karts with her!

We only had one chance left to get into the final, and that was Frankie. But my heart sank when the drivers lined up in their karts, and I saw that she was in the same heat as Weedy Alex, Josh's mate. Alex wasn't quite such a good karter as Josh, but he wasn't bad.

"Come on, Frankie!" I muttered, as the karts revved up, waiting for the flag. It would give us all a boost for the team race tomorrow if one of us got through to the final today.

The race began, and the karts shot away. Frankie didn't get a very good start, so she was only in fourth place as they all completed the first lap. Weedy Alex was first. It was the same for the next three laps. But by the fifth lap, Frankie suddenly began to move up a bit. The driver in front of her didn't take one of the sharp bends very well, and Frankie swept round the side of him, and moved up into third place.

We all cheered and clapped and did loads of high fives. In fact we were so busy doing high fives that we almost missed Frankie moving up into *second* place! She'd put her foot down on the accelerator, and somehow managed to get round the kart right in front of her. Now, on the tenth lap, she was gaining fast on Alex.

"She's going to catch him!" Rosie squealed, grabbing Lyndz round the neck and nearly choking her.

"Come on, Frankie!" Fliss yelled, jumping up and down like a mad thing.

"OW!" That was me. Fliss had just stepped on my toe. "Go, Frankie!"

We all started chanting "Go, Frankie! Go, Frankie! Go, Frankie!" at the top of our voices. There were only two laps to go now, and Alex and Frankie were almost neck and neck. Then Frankie managed to pull level.

"There's only one lap to go!" Lyndz shrieked.

"Don't let him get past you, Frankie," Fliss wailed.

"I can't watch!" I groaned, and buried my head in my hands. 'Course, I went and missed the most exciting bit, didn't I?

"SHE'S OVERTAKEN HIM!" Rosie shouted in my ear. "Look!"

I couldn't believe it. I looked up just in time to see Frankie roar across the finishing line with Alex right behind her. She'd won her heat, and at last we had a Sleepover in the final!

We all went completely crazy. We were hugging each other and slapping each other on the back and jumping up and down, and when Frankie got out of her kart and ran over to us, we started doing it all over again.

"Hey, wait a minute!" Frankie protested, as we all tried to hug her at once. "It was only the heat. I've still got to race in the final!"

"Yeah, but you *won*," Rosie pointed out breathlessly. "You might win the final too!"

Frankie grinned. "Well, I'll have a good try anyway."

I glanced across at Josh Stevens. He looked absolutely furious, and he was giving poor old weedy Alex a good telling-off.

"That really wound Bighead Stevens up," I said with satisfaction. "You can beat him, Frankie, I know you can."

Josh happened to look over at us right at that moment, so we all waved smugly.

"Looks like some girls *are* better at karting than some boys!" I called pointedly.

"Huh! That was just beginner's luck!" Josh snorted. He glared at Frankie. "You don't stand a chance of winning the final."

"We'll see," Frankie said coolly. She didn't look nervous at all. What a star!

That was the last heat, so we didn't have to wait very long before the karts that were in the final were flashed up on the display screen. We all gathered round Frankie to wish her good luck.

"Now watch that bend at the far end of the track," I instructed her. "It can be really tricky."

"And remember, don't look over your shoulder, even if you think someone's about to overtake you," Rosie chimed in anxiously.

Fliss added her bit. "Don't forget not to brake when you go round the corners."

"And don't be nervous," Lyndz said kindly.

"I wasn't before," Frankie replied, picking up her helmet. "But I am now!"

We all slapped palms, and then Frankie went over to her kart. I couldn't sit still as we waited for the race to start. I was jumping around like I had ants in my pants – I wanted her to win *sooo* badly and show Josh Stevens just how stupid he was!

The commentator's voice boomed out of the loudspeaker above our heads. "And the karts are all lined up ready for today's final. I wonder who's going to win?"

"FRANKIE!" the four of us yelled. Everyone looked at us, but we didn't care.

We were all nearly wetting ourselves when the marshall lifted the flag to start the race.

Fliss was hanging on to my arm, and I was holding on to Lyndz's hand, and Rosie was leaning on Lyndz's shoulder. If one of us had tried to move suddenly, we'd *all* have fallen over!

There was a roar of engines as the flag fell, and the karts took off from the starting grid like rockets. We all strained our eyes impatiently to see where Frankie was, and there she was – in front!

"She's beating Josh!" Fliss squealed, looking as if she was about to faint with excitement.

"Calm down, Fliss!" I yelled, even though my own heart was pounding with adrenalin. "There's fourteen laps to go yet!"

"Look at Josh," Rosie said gleefully. "He can't *stand* being behind Frankie!"

She was right. The black and gold kart was on Frankie's tail, and was constantly twisting and weaving, trying to find a way through. But Frankie wasn't letting him. The question was, how long could she hold out?

We soon found out. As they raced towards a hairpin bend, Snooty Stevens made his move. He pulled up alongside Frankie, and, as he did so, he gave her kart a little nudge with his own.

"Did you see that?" I yelled furiously. "He bumped Frankie out of the way! That was a definite foul, ref!"

"Kenny, this isn't a game of footie," Lyndz pointed out.

"I think we should complain!" Fliss muttered, her face red. "Mike said we shouldn't bump into anyone on purpose – it's against the rules."

Our hearts sank right down into our shoes as we watched Josh overtake Frankie on the inside and zoom off into the lead. He waved as he went round her – probably pretending he was apologising, but we all knew he'd done it on purpose.

"Yeah, but Mike also said that sometimes you can't *help* bumping into people," Rosie pointed out. "Smelly Stevens would only say it was an accident."

"And he didn't get a black flag, so he's got away with it," I said, clenching my fists. "Come *on*, Frankie!"

We all fixed our eyes on Frankie's kart, willing her on. If the whole building had collapsed right at that minute, we wouldn't even have noticed!

"She's catching him up!" Fliss shouted suddenly.

Frankie was now right behind Josh Stevens. She was so close their karts were almost touching.

And then it happened.

Suddenly Frankie's kart smashed right into the back of Josh's. Both karts locked together, spun out of control and ended up crashing into the side barriers with a loud BANG!

We all stared with our mouths open for a good few seconds. We just couldn't *believe* it. A couple of the race marshalls had to rush on and pull the karts apart because they were stuck together, and Frankie and Josh Stevens had to leave the track. They were both out of the race.

"What happened?" I asked the others urgently. "It looked like Frankie smashed into Josh on purpose!"

The others were looking as sick as I felt.

"I know," Fliss groaned. "And Frankie *knows* that bumping isn't allowed!"

Frankie and Josh Stevens were standing by the side of the track yelling at each other. We couldn't hear what they were saying, but, from the way they were both waving their arms around, it wasn't nice. We rushed over to them, but before we got there, Josh had stomped off in a complete fury.

"Frankie, are you OK?" Lyndz asked.

"I'm fine," Frankie muttered, although she was as white as a sheet. "Sorry, guys. I really messed up out there."

"Never mind," I said quickly, "As long as you're OK..."

"What happened?" Fliss asked. "Didn't you remember that bumping someone else's kart isn't allowed?"

Frankie looked a bit sheepish. "Yeah, I did... But Josh'd just done it to me, so I thought I'd get him back."

"Get him back!" Rosie said. "You nearly blasted him off the track!"

"Yeah, I don't know how that happened,"

Frankie frowned. "I only meant to give him a little tap. Then next minute – kaboom!"

Just then one of the race marshalls came over to Frankie. "Mike wants to have a word with you," he said.

Frankie groaned. "I bet I'm going to get a right telling-off!" she muttered in my ear.

"Oh, well." I turned to the others and tried to look on the bright side. "At least now we know we've got a great chance in the team races tomorrow, what with Frankie doing so well *before* the crash."

"Yeah, she's our star driver," Lyndz agreed.

"But we're all doing pretty OK," Fliss chimed in.

"Even me!" Rosie added.

Frankie came back over to us. Her face was as long as the wettest weekend ever.

"What's up?" I asked with a frown.

"Josh has complained about my driving," Frankie told us gloomily. "I've been banned from taking part in the team races tomorrow..."

CHAPTER SEVEN

"*WHAT!*" we all shrieked.

"Josh made a right fuss about me being a dangerous driver," Frankie went on. "I tried to tell them I didn't mean to bump him so hard, but they wouldn't listen."

"This just isn't *fair!*" I raged. I glanced over at Josh Stevens, who was standing chatting to his pathetic mates. He looked well pleased with himself, and when he saw me staring, he gave me a smug grin. "I'm finally going to tell that little toad exactly what I think of him!"

"Hold on, Kenny." Frankie grabbed my arm. "If you go and thump Josh, you'll get banned as well!"

"Yeah, Kenny, and we're already one team member down," Rosie pointed out.

I stopped and thought about that. Apart from the fact that Frankie was our best driver, you had to have five people to take part, and now we only had four.

"Maybe we should just drop out of tomorrow's race," Lyndz suggested. "It won't be half such a good laugh without Frankie anyway."

"Yeah, Lyndz is right," Fliss agreed gloomily.

But Frankie was shaking her head. "I don't want you guys to lose out," she said bravely. "If you can find someone else to take my place, you should just go for it."

Just then Charlie came running over to us.

"I just heard about what happened from one of the race marshalls," she said breathlessly. "Bad luck, Frankie. I'm really sorry."

"I didn't mean to bump Josh that hard," Frankie said in a wobbly voice. "I just don't know how it happened."

Charlie frowned. "Well, Josh probably guessed what you were going to do, and put his brakes on slightly, right at the last second. That would mean you'd hit him a lot harder than you thought you would."

"I bet he did that on purpose so he could complain, and get Frankie banned from tomorrow's race!" I said furiously.

"Yeah, and Mike's just given in to Josh because Dad owns the track," Charlie added angrily. "They wouldn't have done it for anyone else."

"What shall we do, Charlie?" Fliss asked anxiously.

"I'll have a go at Josh and see if I can get him to withdraw his complaint," Charlie replied. "But don't hold your breath."

"Couldn't your dad do something?" Lyndz asked hopefully.

"He could, but he's just gone to Hong Kong on business," Charlie sighed. "He won't be back till next week."

"Hey, wait a minute!" I yelled. I had a brill idea. "Charlie, couldn't *you* be in our team instead of Frankie?"

"That's a great idea!" Frankie agreed, looking a lot more cheerful, and the others

84

nodded. It looked like our problem was solved!

But Charlie still looked glum.

"Sorry, folks, I'm too old to race on the junior track," she replied. "But I'll ask around, and see if I can find you someone else. Look, come along tomorrow anyway." She slapped Frankie on the back. "I might be able to persuade Josh to change his mind."

"Yeah, and pigs might fly!" I muttered, as Charlie went off. "What are we going to do now?"

"If you need a driver, I could be in your team tomorrow," said this dozy voice behind us.

We all turned round. Alana Banana was standing there. She must have overheard everything we were saying.

"What?" I spluttered.

"I haven't got a team to race with tomorrow," Alana said helpfully. "I could take Frankie's place."

"Aren't you racing with your brother?" Rosie asked.

"Kevin doesn't want me in his team." Alana looked puzzled. "I don't know why."

"I can take a guess!" I muttered to Fliss.

"Well?" Alana Banana looked at us eagerly. "Am I in or what?"

"Over my dead body—" I began, but I shut up when Lyndz nudged me in the ribs.

"Er – we'll let you know, Alana," Fliss said quickly.

Alana Banana nodded, and wandered off, bumping right into one of the other drivers and nearly knocking him over.

I groaned. "She can hardly drive *herself* in a straight line, let along a kart!"

"But if we can't get anyone else…" Fliss didn't finish the sentence.

She was right. Either we got Frankie back into the team, or we had to go with whoever else might be free to take part when we arrived at the track tomorrow. And that just might mean dopey Alana Banana Palmer…

"Well, what about Callum?" Fliss said, for the sixth time. "He might be OK."

"He's a bit young," I said doubtfully. "And he's a bit – well, you know…"

"A bit what?" Fliss's eyes started flashing

dangerously. I'd been about to say that Fliss's brother was a bit weedy – even weedier than Alex and Robin, in fact – but I decided not to. We were all feeling stressed out, and I didn't want to start a row with Fliss.

It was quite late at night, and we were round at Lyndz's house for our sleepover. We were supposed to be having a great old time, making our T-shirts and discussing race tactics, but instead we were sitting around in Lyndz's bedroom being miserable. We'd started off being really positive. We'd even started painting our T-shirts with fabric paint. We'd done silver stars round the necklines, and a big purple heart in the middle. Then we were going to write *Sleepover Club Forever!* underneath in silver paint – until Fliss pointed out that whoever took Frankie's place wouldn't be a Sleepover Club member. That had depressed us in a major way, so we'd left the T-shirts half-finished.

"I was just going to say that Callum's a bit inexperienced," I said, crawling over Lyndz's bed to grab a Wispa bar. We were having our midnight feast and we were all starving because we'd been too depressed to eat much dinner. "You said he's never karted before."

"Yeah, but at the moment he's our only hope," Fliss pointed out.

She was right. Callum was the only one of our brothers and sisters who was under eleven, but old enough to take part.

"Maybe Charlie can persuade Josh to let Frankie race," Lyndz said hopefully. She had her black kitten, Zebedee, on her lap and he was purring away like an engine.

"No way," I said. "Josh knows we've got a great chance of winning the team race with Frankie. Without her, we're dead."

"No, you're not," Frankie butted in. She was lying on the floor, eating a Snickers bar. "You might turn up at the track tomorrow and find someone really brilliant to be in the team."

"Like who?" I snorted. "Anyone who's any good will be in a team already. No, we're more likely to end up with someone who's never raced before, or a complete dork."

"Like Alana Banana," Rosie muttered.

"We might as well not bother entering the race if we have to go with Alana Banana," I said firmly. "I'd rather let Zebedee drive for us!"

"Maybe we just shouldn't bother turning up tomorrow," Fliss suggested.

"That might be the best thing," I agreed. I couldn't *bear* to think of Josh Stevens being all smug because he'd beaten us.

"But what if Charlie's found someone else to be in our team?" Lyndz pointed out.

We all sighed. We just couldn't make our minds up.

"I think we should vote on it," Frankie suggested. "Let's write down what we think in our diaries."

So we all grabbed our Sleepover diaries and got writing. Then we passed them round and read each other's. Lyndz's was covered in cat hairs, and read:

I think we should go to the track tomorrow just in case Charlie's persuaded Josh to change his mind. And if she hasn't, we're sure to find someone else to be in our team. It won't be the same as having Frankie, though.

Mine said:

> If Frankie's not in our team, I can't see much point in taking part. I mean, we're supposed to be the Sleepover Club team. But if everyone else wants to go, I will.

Fliss's said:

> I think we should definitely ask Callum. But if he's rubbish, then I'll get the blame. Maybe we shouldn't go at all. Oh, I don't know... Help!

Rosie's was:

> I think we should go to the track tomorrow and find another driver. Charlie can help us to get someone good, not dopey Alana Banana.

And Frankie wrote:

> I'd feel really bad if everyone pulled out of the race because of me. I think you should give it a go.

So it was three votes to two. We were going to take part in that team race, with or without Frankie.

"Looks like we're gonna be back at the track tomorrow then, folks," I said slowly.

The others all looked at me solemnly and nodded.

"Let's just hope we find someone good to take Frankie's place…"

CHAPTER EIGHT

"How did you get on, Charlie?"

"Did you find us another driver?"

"Did you talk to Josh?"

"Is he going to let Frankie race?"

"What did the little creep say?" (That was me.)

We'd just arrived at the track the following morning, and the minute we spotted Charlie, we rushed over to her. But one look at her face told us the news wasn't good.

"Sorry, girls," she muttered, looking embarrassed. "I did my best, but he won't withdraw that complaint. He was saying something about salt in a glass of Coke?"

I turned pink. "Yeah, well, he deserved it."

"So now we've got to see about getting you another driver," Charlie said briskly. "I've asked around some of my mates, but all their younger brothers and sisters are already in teams."

"So what are we going to do?" Fliss wailed.

"Watch the practice sessions before the races," Charlie advised us. "Then you can see which drivers are good, and ask them if they'd be interested in joining your team. And I'll keep asking around, OK?"

We all nodded gloomily. We hadn't really expected Charlie to persuade Josh, but I guess we'd all been secretly hoping that she would. Now we knew for sure that Frankie wasn't going to be taking part, we all felt a bit sick.

"Oh, well, I didn't really think Snooty Stevens would back down," Frankie remarked, trying not to sound gutted as Charlie hurried off.

"No," we all agreed sadly.

To make things worse, Alana Banana

suddenly appeared, and wandered over to us.

"Hi," she said dozily. "Have you found someone to take Frankie's place yet?"

"No," I muttered. If Alana Banana was the only person at the track that morning who wasn't in a team, we'd either have to have her in ours or go home without competing. Either way, Josh Stevens would be laughing his head off.

"Oh," Alana shrugged. "Well, I just came to tell you I can't race with you. I'm going to be in Kevin's team after all, because one of his mates dropped out."

"He must be pleased," I whispered to Frankie. We both looked across at Kevin Palmer, who was stomping around in what looked like a complete sulk. I think I'd have been the same if I'd had to have useless Alana Banana on my team!

"Well, that's one problem solved at least!" Fliss breathed a sigh of relief as Alana drifted away.

"Look, the first practice session's starting." Rosie pointed at the track. "We'd better go and check it out."

"Hang on a minute…" A brilliant plan had just popped right into my head. "I've got an idea!"

The others didn't react *quite* like I was hoping.

"Not another of your mad ideas, Kenny!" Frankie groaned.

"I hope you're not going to attack Josh Stevens," Fliss said sternly.

"Then we'd *all* get banned from the race," Rosie added.

"Just forget about it, Kenny," Lyndz suggested.

"You lot are weedier than Alex and Robin!" I grumbled. "This is a great idea – and it might just work. Follow me!"

I marched over to where Josh Stevens was standing with Alex and Robin, plus two other guys who had to be his other team-mates, Ben and Nathan. They had exactly the same weedy look as the other two. The others reluctantly followed me, muttering amongst themselves. I think they were sorting out a back-up plan in case I attacked Snotty Stevens!

But it wasn't violence I had in mind – not this time anyway! I went straight up to Josh, who looked pretty surprised to see me.

"Hello, girlies!" he sneered. "I didn't expect to see *you* again after your pathetic attempt to beat me yesterday."

"Oh, we're not giving up," I retorted, keeping my cool even though my blood was boiling. "We still think we've got a pretty good chance in the race, even without Frankie."

Snooty Stevens laughed. "What makes you think that?"

I went in for the kill. "Well, *you* obviously thought we could beat your team – that's why you deliberately got Frankie chucked out of the race. You were scared we'd beat you, so you set us up!"

I knew that was probably true, but I was secretly hoping that Josh would immediately deny it, get mad and say Frankie *could* take part in the race and he'd beat us fair and square. My dad calls it *reverse psychology*!

Josh had turned red with fury. "That's a load of rubbish!" he declared. Then suddenly he started laughing himself silly. "Hey, I know what you're up to. You're playing mind-games…"

"It's reverse psychology," put in Alex, who obviously wasn't as stupid as he looked.

"Yeah, you want me to get mad and say *OK, let her race, and I'll beat you all.*" Josh grinned mockingly at me. "Well, tough! Because I'm not going to."

OK, so I'd been rumbled. It was our last shot, and I'd run out of ideas.

"Come on, let's get out of here," I muttered to the others, my face bright red.

"Hang on a minute," Snotty Stevens called after us, as we sloped off. "You really want Frankie to take part in that race, don't you? Well, maybe she can…"

That made us all turn round.

"If this is a stupid trick, I'm gonna thump him this time, and no-one's going to stop me!" I growled, as Josh strolled over to us.

"I've been thinking," he began. I didn't like the look of the nasty gleam in his eyes. "Maybe I *will* go to Mike and ask him to let Frankie race."

"Why would you do that?" I asked suspiciously. There just *had* to be a catch.

There was.

"OK, here's the deal." Josh hooked his thumbs into the waistband of his combat trousers in a pathetic effort to look cool. "I'll get Frankie back into the race, but if my team beats yours, you stay off this track from now on…"

I was a bit surprised as I looked at the others. That sounded OK. I mean, we all enjoyed karting, but it was quite expensive if you didn't have free passes, so we weren't sure how often we'd come back anyway. Besides, there were other karting centres we could go to if we wanted.

"OK?" I raised my eyebrows at the others, and they all nodded. I turned to Josh.

"All right," I agreed, hardly believing we were getting off so lightly. "We'll stay away from the centre if you beat us."

"Hang on…" Snooty Stevens gave us an evil grin. "I didn't say I wanted you to keep away from the *centre*. Just to stay off the *track*."

We all looked really confused.

"But why would we bother coming here if we can't race?" Frankie asked, puzzled.

"Oh, you'll be here all right," Josh replied

airily. "As my cheerleading squad!"

We all stared at him in amazement.

"Your *what*?" I roared.

"Yep, I fancy having a cheerleading squad to support me when I'm racing," Josh explained smugly. "You'd have to sort out a uniform. You could have T-shirts with my name printed on the front or something."

"You're joking!" Lyndz's mouth had dropped open.

"And you'd have to jump up and down and cheer me while I'm racing," Josh went on, ignoring her. "And if you could dance like Britney Spears, that'd be good."

"You're not *serious*!" Frankie spluttered.

"Yeah, I am." Smarmy Stevens grinned at us. "I go to loads of race meetings, and no-one's got cheerleaders. I'd be the first!"

"That's it!" I charged forward. "Let me at him!"

Everyone rushed in between us right at that moment, so Smarmy Stevens just about got away in one piece.

"That's my offer," he yelled from behind the rest of his team-mates. "Take it or leave it!"

"We'll leave it, thanks very much," Frankie began, but stopped when I grabbed her arm.

"Hang on a sec, Franks. Let's think about this."

"*What?*" the others all said together, staring at me.

"Well, why not?" I'd calmed down a bit, and I was thinking things out. "We've got a great chance of winning with Frankie back on our team."

"But what if we lose?" Frankie pointed out in a tragic voice. "We'll be Smarty-pants Stevens' cheerleaders – we'll look like a bunch of twits!"

"I'd quite like to be a cheerleader," Fliss remarked. "But not for *him*," she added hastily, as we all glared at her.

"We'll win," I said confidently. "So, are we in?" I looked round at everyone. "Or are we out?"

After a moment or two, everyone nodded. I turned back to Josh.

"All right," I snapped. "We accept your offer!"

"Cool." Josh and his mates began sniggering.

"See you on the race track."

"Yeah, you will," I said coldly. "Because we'll all be in front of you!"

Just then Charlie came hurrying over to us.

"I thought you were going to watch the practice sessions," she began. Then she spotted Josh and frowned. "What're you up to *now*, Joshua Roland Stevens?"

"*Roland!*" I spluttered, and we all howled with laughter as Charlie winked at us. Even Alex and the others were smirking.

"Actually, I'm just about to go and talk to Mike," Josh snapped, his face bright red. "I'm going to withdraw my complaint about Frankie."

Charlie looked totally amazed as Josh went off, surrounded by his team-mates. "Oh, that's brilliant!" she gasped.

"Yeah, but things aren't quite that simple," I said grimly, and explained what would happen if we lost. Charlie looked stunned.

"That little creep!" she said crossly. "That's just like him." Then her eyes narrowed, and she grinned. "Well, we'd better make sure he doesn't win then, hadn't we? Come on."

And she hurried off across the arena. Curiously we all followed her outside to where the karts were parked behind the building.

"Here we are!" Charlie pulled off the tarpaulin which was covering *Silver Flash*, and we all gasped. Charlie had finished the painting, and the kart looked fantastic. "It's all yours, Frankie," she went on.

"You mean…?" Frankie gasped.

"Yep, you can drive *Silver Flash* in the team races today," Charlie said with a grin. "All you've got to do now is win!"

Frankie couldn't believe her luck – and neither could the rest of us!

"It's a shame we haven't got our team T-shirts with us," Rosie said. "The purple and silver would have gone really well with *Silver Flash*."

Fliss grinned at us. "Just call me a genius!" she said modestly. She put her hand in her bag, and pulled out – the team T-shirts! And she'd finished them off too, painting *Sleepover Club Forever!* underneath the purple hearts.

"I got up early this morning when the rest of you were still asleep, and finished them off," Fliss confessed. "Just in case! And look…" She delved into her bag again, and pulled out a tube of silver hair mascara.

We all cheered.

"Yes!" I exclaimed. "The Sleepover Club is back in business!"

"Now listen up, all of you," Charlie said, as we gathered round her in a huddle like a team of American football players. "Josh has got quite a few tricks up his sleeve that you need to know about."

We all nodded solemnly. It was nearly time for the races to start, and we were already kitted up with our race suits open at the front so that everyone could see our T-shirts. We all had a silver streak in our hair too – we looked fab!

We were really hyped up about the races, but we knew that Charlie would give us some really good advice, so we were trying to listen hard. She'd just brought *Silver Flash* into the arena, and the look on Josh's face when he'd realised that Frankie was going to be driving Charlie's kart made us all laugh our heads off.

"OK, Josh can be a bit of a bully on the track," Charlie began, and I rolled my eyes. *That* was no surprise. "He'll do everything he can to get past you if you're in front of him. When you're coming up to a corner, he'll try to cut in on you, even if there's no room for him to overtake. What he wants you to do is back off and let him slip through. So you *don't*."

"What if we crash, though?" Lyndz asked.

"You won't," Charlie said confidently. "Josh will pull back at the very last minute, but only if he thinks you won't give way."

"What else?" I asked.

"He likes to try and confuse you about which side he's going to overtake you on a corner," Charlie went on. "So he'll keep moving over to the outside of one of the bends on every lap. Then when you suss out what he's doing and you move to the outside of the bend to block him, he'll overtake you on the inside."

"Sneaky!" Frankie remarked.

Charlie gave us loads more useful advice. She was still talking when the start of the races was announced over the loudspeaker. This was it. Now we were on our own.

"Good luck," Charlie said, slapping me on the back. "I'll be cheering for you all!"

"Thanks, Coach!" I grinned.

There were eight teams taking part, and we'd all be driving in two races each. Everyone would get points, depending on where they finished. I was going in the first race for us, along with Robin from Josh's team and six other competitors. I couldn't help feeling a bit sick as everyone went over to their karts. I didn't usually get nervous, but I *really* wanted to do well this time.

"Welcome to the Silver Streak karting centre for our very first day of team racing!" The commentator's voice boomed out over the loudspeaker. "And before we start, can I just say good luck to one of our teams who go by the name, the Sleepover Club?"

I almost jumped out of my skin. I wasn't expecting that at all! The crowd started cheering and clapping, and so I waved at them and took a bow. I don't know why the commentator had singled us out like that – maybe he thought we were bound to win?

"A little bird tells me that these brave girls have made a bet with boys' team, the Kings of the Track," the commentator went on. "And if the girls lose, they've got to be Josh Stevens's cheerleaders!"

Everyone burst out laughing, and I nearly turned purple with embarrassment. I glanced over at the others, who were all red in the face and trying to hide behind each other. That little toad Stevens must be spreading it all around the track! That meant we couldn't go back on the bet if we lost... Unless we never came to the track again. But anyway, Alana Banana Palmer would be bound to tell the M&Ms. It'd be all over Cuddington Primary in minutes.

I gritted my teeth. There was nothing else for it –we *had* to win!

* * *

I dunno what came over me when the race started, but I went for it. I scorched out of the starting grid like I had a rocket up my bottom – none of the other eight karts had a chance! Fifteen laps later I crossed the finishing line miles ahead of Robin, who was second. What a start!

'Course, we were all celebrating like mad when I came off the track, but we didn't have a lot of time because the race marshalls wanted to get on to the next race. Next up was Fliss, and she was racing against Alex, along with, amongst others, Alana Banana.

Guess what?

Fliss came first too!!!

She had a really difficult race because she and Alex were neck and neck most of the time, but she just about managed to get across the line ahead of him. Class! And guess who came last?

No, you don't get a prize for saying Alana Banana did. She's so dozy, I don't think she even realised it was a race!

"Look, we're winning!" Frankie said gleefully,

as the team's scores flashed up on to the display board. We were, too! We were ahead of Josh's team by two points.

"It's me next," Rosie wailed, looking scared to death. "And Josh is in my race!"

"Look, don't panic," Lyndz said. "You don't have to beat him, just do your best."

"Yeah, remember what Charlie said," I reminded her. "All the points count."

Rosie did do her best, but she was never going to catch Snooty Stevens. She did OK, though – she came third. But Josh came in first, which meant that the boys were catching up with us.

I nudged Frankie when the scores came up again on the display board. "Look, we're level," I said anxiously. "We really need to get a few wins in now, and pull ahead."

"It's Lyndz next," Frankie said, "and she's up against Nathan."

"Don't worry," Lyndz said calmly, putting on her helmet. "His horse isn't as fast as mine!"

We all watched with our hearts in our mouths as the fourth race began. Lyndz did really well, but she didn't win. She did come second though – and luckily for us, Nathan finished behind her in third place. Phew! That meant our score was higher than the boys again.

"I'm so nervous!" Fliss complained, pacing to and fro as we waited for the fifth race to start. "It's driving me mad!" She brightened up a bit. "Hey, *driving* me mad – get it?"

We all groaned.

"Come on, Frankie," I muttered, as we watched her climb into *Silver Flash*, ready to start the race. "You can do it!"

Silver Flash stood out against all the other boring karts in the race – it really looked fantastic. Frankie was going against Ben this time. If we could just win it, our lead over the boys would be even bigger.

We all waited in silence for the marshall's flag to drop. Then, when it did, we started screaming our heads off.

"Go, Frankie!"

"Go, *Silver Flash*!"

"Come on, Sleepover Club!"

Not that Frankie actually *needed* us to yell for her – she was doing all right on her own!

Silver Flash shot into the lead from the start, and nobody could catch her. She completed the fifteen laps as if she was on the track on her own, and cruised over the finishing line in first place while everyone else still had half of the last lap to complete. The best thing was, Ben only finished in fourth place. The first five races were over, and we were four points ahead of the boys!

We were all getting really excited and doing lots of woo-hooing at this point. Charlie kept trying to calm us down.

"There's still five races to go," she kept saying. "Anything can happen."

And you've guessed it. It did.

I think it was me who put everyone off. I was zooming round the track in my second race, when I misjudged a corner badly. I spun right off the track and hit the barrier, and half of the other karts, including Alex, swept past me.

I was really mad with myself. I managed to get my kart going again, and I guess I did pretty well to come in fourth after all that. Luckily Alex didn't win, but he did come second, which cut our lead down to two points.

After that, everything seemed to go a bit pear-shaped. Lyndz could only manage third place in her second race, while Robin was second, and Fliss just about managed to hang on for second place in the next race ahead of Nathan. Then Rosie went against Ben and came fourth, while Ben was second. That meant trouble.

"We're level again," I groaned, as the display board flashed up the latest figures. "I don't believe it!"

And there was only one race left.

Frankie versus Josh. And whoever finished in front of the other, their team would win the prize.

"It's all down to you, Frankie," Rosie said solemnly.

"And *Silver Flash*," Frankie replied. She looked a bit sick, and I didn't blame her.

We all watched in silence as the eight karts lined up for the very last race. All the members of the other teams and the spectators were wittering on, saying how exciting it was that it was so close for the final race. But we didn't think it was exciting at all. We were all wetting ourselves!

We soon cheered up when the race started. Frankie swooped off the starting grid, and took the lead immediately in *Silver Flash*!

"Yes!" Rosie yelled. "Keep going, Frankie!"

"You can do it, Frankie!" Lyndz shouted.

"Oh, I can't watch!" Fliss moaned, and covered her eyes. But half a second later she was glued to the track again.

I was glad Frankie was in the lead, of course, but as the race settled down, I began to feel a bit worried. Josh wasn't challenging Frankie for first place. He seemed quite happy to stay behind her in second, and just keep watching and waiting for the right moment to overtake. But when was he going to do it?

Ten, eleven, twelve, thirteen laps. There were only two laps left, and Frankie was still just about in the lead. We were all hoarse from cheering too much, and Josh was still in second place.

And THEN it happened.

Alana Banana was right at the back of everyone else. In fact, she was so slow that Frankie was about to lap her, but Alana was blocking her way. The marshall started signalling to Alana to pull over. Guess what? She's such a dozy idiot, she just waved back at him!

Anyway, it took about a minute or two before Alana Banana realised what was happening, and then she pulled over – right into Frankie's path! Frankie had to brake to avoid her, and guess who shot through the gap like an arrow and took the lead?

Josh flippin' Stevens, that's who!

CHAPTER TEN

The whole crowd gasped, but the rest of the Sleepover Club and Charlie were speechless. Josh was in front – with one lap to go!

"I'm gonna kill Alana Banana!" I yelled, stomping up and down in a rage. "She's a stupid, dozy, dopey idiot! You wait till I see her at school next week—"

"Frankie's catching Josh up!" Rosie shrieked in my ear.

"What!"

Sure enough, *Silver Flash* was gaining ground on the black and gold kart.

"If Frankie's brave enough to go for it,

Silver Flash has got the speed to do it," muttered Charlie, who'd chewed her fingernails nearly down to the bone.

"Oh, Frankie's got the guts to do it," I said confidently. "No problem!"

But would she have the time? There was only half a lap left.

We all clung on to each other as *Silver Flash* drew up behind Josh's kart. Fliss was hanging on to my hand so hard her fingernails were digging into me, but I hardly noticed. Rosie and Lyndz were jumping up and down, holding on to each other. Half a lap to go…

Less than half a lap…

Suddenly Frankie seemed to put her foot down and find an extra burst of speed. She revved up her engine and shot past Josh, taking him by surprise. Next second the silver nose of Charlie's kart was crossing the finishing line. We'd done it!

"Yee-hah!" I yelled, leaping on top of the others and almost crushing them. "We beat them – by one point!"

We all went mad, hugging each other and Charlie, and dancing round in circles and punching the air. Thank goodness we were saved from being girly cheerleaders for Snotty Stevens – it was a miracle!

"And the winner is – Francesca Thomas for the Sleepover Club team," the commentator boomed out. "Which means that they are our winners today by one point over the Kings of the Track. Well done, girls – but I think you'd have made great cheerleaders!"

When Frankie rushed over to us, we all leapt on *her*, and nearly crushed *her* to bits.

"You were fab, Francesca Thomas!" I announced, slapping her on the back and nearly knocking her over.

"Yeah, class, Frankie," Rosie agreed, giving her a friendly punch on the arm.

"We knew you wouldn't let us down," Fliss chimed in, giving Frankie a hug which nearly choked her.

"You deserve a special champion's sleepover tonight," Lyndz suggested, punching her on the other arm.

"Thanks," Frankie grinned modestly. "But it was all down to *Silver Flash* really." She looked around. "Where's Charlie?"

Then we saw her. She was holding Josh's arm and pulling him towards us, while they argued furiously.

"I think Josh has got something to say to you," Charlie said, giving her brother a shove.

"Ow!" Josh said sullenly.

We all waited. It was ace to see Snotty Stevens red in the face, looking like he wished he was a million miles away!

"Well?" Charlie raised her eyebrows.

"They only won because they had *Silver Flash*," Josh muttered furiously.

"You can't have it both ways, Josh," Charlie pointed out calmly. "Either Frankie's a great driver, or your sister's a great mechanic."

"Either way, us girls win!" I announced gleefully.

Josh glared at me, but we weren't about to let him off the hook. "OK," he admitted reluctantly. "Maybe *some* girls are not too bad at karting…"

"Not too bad!" we all chorused scornfully.

"All right, some girls are *good* at karting,"

Josh muttered. "But I bet I can beat you in the individual races next!"

"Says who?" I began crossly, but Frankie and Charlie looked at each other and nodded. Charlie took Josh's arm and pulled him away, and Frankie blocked my path so I couldn't go after him.

"No, Kenny," she said firmly. "I think we've had enough excitement for one day!"

"Not quite," Fliss said. "It's time to collect our prizes!"

"I've never won a gold medal before!" I said, examining it for about the millionth time. "It's so cool!"

It was later that day, and we were round at Fliss's, in the Proudloves' garden. Actually, we'd been round *all* our houses, showing off our medals. Everyone was dead impressed. We'd ended up at the Proudloves because Fliss had invited us all for tea, although I don't think her mum was too pleased when she found out.

"Show us again how you beat Josh, Frankie," Lyndz said.

Frankie didn't need asking twice. She'd already acted out her victory race for us at least three times.

"OK, so this is the start of the race." Frankie charged down the garden and positioned herself near a tree. "I knew I had to get a good start to get ahead of Josh."

"Did you feel nervous?" Rosie asked.

"You bet!" Frankie replied. "I knew Kenny would kill me if I lost."

"Ha ha," I said.

"I'm not joking!" Frankie winked at me. "Anyway, the race started, and I couldn't believe I was out in front."

She zoomed up the garden towards us, turning an imaginary steering wheel. "Josh was trying to get past me at first, and then he stopped. I got a bit worried, but I just concentrated on staying in front."

Fliss came out of the house just then, carrying a tray with some glasses on it and a mega-sized bottle of lemonade.

"What happened then?" I asked.

"Well, I could see that Alana Banana was going to be in my way because she wasn't going fast enough," Frankie went on. "I was just waiting for her to move – and then she went and blocked my path. I was really stressed out! Josh overtook me, but I put my foot down –" she ran up the garden and flopped into one of the chairs – "and I just managed to catch him!"

We all cheered.

"Hey, I've got a great idea." I grabbed the big bottle of lemonade, and began shaking it up. "You know what the racing drivers do with champagne, don't you?"

"No, Kenny!" the others shrieked, as I loosened the top of the bottle.

The lemonade shot out in this massive spray which went *everywhere*. We all got soaked!

And so did Mr Watson-Wade, whose angry, dripping wet face appeared over the fence right at that moment. He'd been weeding the flowerbed near the fence and got in the way...

Oops! Time for me to put my foot down and zoom off, I think. See ya!

40

Sleepover Girls Go Wild!

The Sleepover Club is off to the local wildlife park, Animal World, for the day! Will Frankie enter the Spider House? Will Fliss go anywhere near the snakes? But then Kenny starts teasing Lyndz about what Hissing Horace the python's having for supper. Little does she know what she's started...

Pack up your sleepover kit and let's PIG OUT!

Collins

41

The Sleepover Club at the Carnival

Carnival is coming to Cuddington! Frankie and her mates do loads of research for their carnival float – and things get seriously interesting when they stumble on some old wartime photos of the village. Who's that girl, the one who looks exactly like Kenny? Is it coincidence, or could they be related?

Dress yourself up and groove on over!

The Sleepover Club on the Beach

A long weekend of camping by the seaside offers a few surprises for the Sleepover Club. Their first surprise is that there are no funfairs or arcades near the campsite – boring! But then they find a mysterious message in a bottle, washed up by the tide...

Roll up your combats and paddle on over!

www.harpercollins.co.uk
Visit the book lover's website

Order Form

To order direct from the publishers, just make a list of the titles you want and fill in the form below:

Name ....

Address ....

....

....

Send to: Dept 6, HarperCollins Publishers Ltd, Westerhill Road, Bishopbriggs, Glasgow G64 2QT.

Please enclose a cheque or postal order to the value of the cover price, plus:

UK & BFPO: Add £1.00 for the first book, and 25p per copy for each additional book ordered.

Overseas and Eire: Add £2.95 service charge. Books will be sent by surface mail but quotes for airmail despatch will be given on request.

A 24-hour telephone ordering service is available to holders of Visa, MasterCard, Amex or Switch cards on 0141- 772 2281.

Collins
An *Imprint of* HarperCollins*Publishers*